HEART'S REST

God's Gift To
A Grieving Parent

By Kathryn Popio

Fairway Press
Lima, Ohio

HEART'S REST

FIRST EDITION
Copyright © 1992 by
Kathryn Popio

Scripture quotations are from the: *Revised Standard Version of the Bible*, copyrighted 1946, 1952, ©, 1971, 1973, by the Division of Christian Education of the National Council of the Churches of Christ in the USA, used by permission; and the *King James Version of the Bible*, in the public domain.

Revised Standard Version, Thomas Nelson & Sons, N.Y., 1952.
1. Table of Contents verse: Romans 10:17
2. Chapter 1: 1 Thessalonians 4:13-14
3. Chapter 7: Matthew 18:18

Other sources:
1. Claudia Jewett's work (p. 24) *Helping Children Cope With Separation and Loss*, © 1982, The Boston Common Press, Massachusetts. Used by permission.
2. Abraham Maslow's work (p. 60) *The Farther Reaches of Human Nature*, The Viking Press, New York, © 1971. Used by permission.
3. Kathryn Popio's poem (p. 54) "Child's Play," © 1985; First appeared in "alive now!" published by *The Upper Room*, Nashville, Tennessee, Vol. 15, No. 4.

7912 / ISBN 1-55673-457-3   PRINTED IN U.S.A.

Dedicated,
to all those other parents
who have lost a son or a daughter.
I'm writing this *for you* . . .
because of *God's* precious son,
Jesus Christ.

Table Of Contents

Preface 9

1 Reaching Across 13

2 A Place To Grieve 21

3 Grief Peaks 31

4 Doing The Next Thing Again And Again 39

5 A Time For Putting Away 47

6 Being Your Own Good Friend 55

7 Next To The Last Chapter 63

So faith comes from what is heard, and what is heard comes by the preaching of Christ.
— Romans 10:17

Acknowledgements

My not-quite-intact manuscript first went to my two dear scrutinizers, Martha J. Petersen and Marcia Hinds. Their critical suggestions and loving encouragement helped me to organize the still not-quite-perfect editions that followed.

In its improved form, *Heart's Rest* then went through an extensive review by Rev. Paul Richard Williams. After his editing pen cooled down, Bill and Lonnie Dearth, Roberta A. Martin, Judy Hardgrove, Jean R. Linderman, and Dianne M. Peecook provided me with much-needed verification of this work's potential for outreach to other parents, ministers and seminary students.

I also sought appraisal by Kathleen L. Casey, Edmund Siennicki, Judy A. Totts, Janet L. Welch, Betty L. Wetzel, and Sandra Fahning before this piece of work reached its destination at Fairway Press.

The enthusiastic expertise of the staff at Fairway Press — Ellen Shockey, Fred Steiner, and Sarah Macpherson — made the final processes of editing, designing and marketing run smoothly to the finish. And during that time, Jim Lovejoy succeeded in giving vitality to the cover of *Heart's Rest* by combining the work of Marcia Lincoln Hinds, his own brand of artistic ingenuity, and the brilliant blue that was Mac's favorite color. The cover portrait also shows an original piece of music written in memory of Mac for the Medina County Honors Band by Edmund J. Siennicki. Commissioned by Marcus Neiman, it was premiered by the Medina Community Band and Medina Honors Band in 1989 under the title, "M.P. March." During the process of publishing, the title has been changed to "Macaulay's March."

Last, but not least, I am grateful for the consulting expertise of Joan R. Long, R.N., of High Point, North Carolina and for Heather and Pete's invaluable support for my project.

It was not easy for any of these people to offer critical comments on a topic like bereavement; yet, they each were gracious enough and brave enough to step forward and give me the honest feedback I needed in order to help others with their grief. So, in this small voice, I thank each of these people for their unique contributions toward the wholeness of *Heart's Rest* and for their supportive comments, lunches, coffees, hugs and prayers.

K.P.

Preface

This is an account of my journey through the grieving process; a journey with God holding my arm and continually making it possible to face what had to be faced at the time my son, Macaulay, left this life when he had just turned thirteen and entered his new existence.

Aside from the first night, I have slept at least a portion of every night. That fact, in itself, surprises people. It surprises me, even now. I mention it, because it indicates the peace I was given from the very beginning and which has prevailed throughout the mourning process.

Mourning . . . and peace. They sound contradictory at first. Yet, in the midst of the suffering that took our son (brother, grandson, nephew, cousin . . . friend), we were immediately allowed to witness God's promise of eternal life being realized. And that has made all the difference in the way we have been able to continue each day since then. As I tell of the events that have been our lives for the past several years, those two words — mourning and peace — will grow more compatible.

It has always seemed *right* that our gift should be shared. Seeing God's Grace touch others by my willingness to do so has helped me speak about it another time and yet another. While I will probably never understand "the why" of that bicycle-car accident which brought an end to Mac's earthly life, this is my personal account of how our Lord allowed Mac's *spirit* to reach out at the instant of death with *a hint* of the magnificence of the new existence he was entering. That experience, in itself, is sufficiently sustaining and hope-filled. Yet, I will also relate other ways that our Father has reached out with such tender touches that I could never begin to adequately describe His healing at work in my own spirit, as well. Of course, individuals mourn in their unique ways; according to their personality, background and relationship with God. Therefore, this book is my personal experience with God's Grace, and it is my belief that such unique care is intended for us all.

Kathryn Popio
February 1992

1 Thessalonians 4:13-14

"But we would not have you ignorant,
brethren, concerning those who are asleep,
that you may not grieve as others do
who have no hope. For since we believe
Jesus died and rose again, even so,
THROUGH JESUS, God will bring with Him
those who have fallen asleep."

1
Reaching Across

The week before Mac died, he brought an unusual kaleido-scope to my attention. We had gone to a friend's autograph party at the mall book store. As I stood talking, Mac busied himself looking around at the displays at the front of the store. He was always calling me to share things that had absorbed his attention. That afternoon was typical.

"Hey, look through this," he urged, when he was able to get a word into the conversation. He had a kaleidoscope in his hand, and he held it up for me to take a peek. "Look at all the different designs it makes against your skirt and the floor and *every color* you show it against!"

It was an unusual optical instrument, indeed. Instead of having colored chips inside allowing predictable patterns, the glass shapes were crystal. Every background you held it against changed the designs immensely. One of our friends wore black which made a magnificent display. Cream was beautiful. It made looking into the book shop an exhilarating experience. In essence, it altered reality for a few seconds by making it beautifully multifaceted. We all took a peek, trying it against the various backgrounds and colors. Then I returned it to Mac and resumed my conversations while he continued experimenting.

I didn't recall that experience again until I came across a smaller version of a crystal kaleidoscope at another shop nearly a year later; nor did I realize what a gorgeous moment Macaulay had drawn me into that day. Of course, I bought that small kaleidoscope; for now, in his absence, it repeatedly pointed out that the ability to create beautiful patterns in life is infinite. In fact, through God's Grace, it was at the precise moment Mac left his life here with us that I got my first glimpse of some of the dimensions life really offers to us all.

The accident happened about 5:08 in the evening, August 22, 1988. Mac had peeled potatoes for me and went out to ride his bike while supper was cooking. I will never forget those three loud bangs on the aluminum storm door followed by "Mac's been hit by a car!"

The rescue squad was called, and they came within minutes. Since the paramedics wanted to work with Mac, they wouldn't allow me to ride in the ambulance with him. Our neighbor, Bill, who first realized Mac had been hit, drove my husband, Pete, and me to the hospital in Wadsworth that was ten minutes away. Our daughter Heather stayed home to notify family and our minister in Akron, who lived about thirty minutes from the hospital. Bill prayed out loud for us all the way to the hospital. I remember his prayers — that people would be there to provide immediate care for Mac, and that the needs of our family would also be met. It was comforting to know he was praying because by that time, I was riding along in silent shock.

Pete and Bill and I arrived at the hospital at about 5:25. At the front desk, they took the least information possible before taking us to a back room where Pete and I were seated on a couch. Bill pulled up a chair directly across from us, held our hands and continued to pray quietly. The doctor came into the room soon thereafter to speak with us.

14

He said, "Right off the bat, I'll tell you that your son is brain-dead. But his heart is still beating, and as long as it is, we will work with that."

I couldn't speak. I sat in a daze. After that initial briefing, the doctor came in every fifteen minutes or so to report that there was no change. Nothing was happening in the way of a response. The three of us continued sitting in that small room . . . two of us in shock and the other silently praying.

All of a sudden, I heard Mac's voice call with great excitement and joy, "Hey, Mom! Hey, Mom!"

I quickly looked up at the wall in response to his voice. Nothing was there. Then I turned my head a little more to the right to look at the clock on the wall. It was 6:19.

As I began turning my head back to my original position, a wonderful peace and comfort enveloped me. When next I looked at Bill's face, he was beaming with joy! He was literally beaming with happiness, and he said, "What is it, Kathie? What did you hear?"

I told him I had heard Mac.

As we continued to sit in silence, I felt some kind of energy in my brain. That is the only way I can describe it. While I did not hear anything else, I must have felt like I might; after that, my blank staring ceased. I began glancing around the room as if trying to listen for more. But I didn't hear anything more.

When the doctor came in about fifteen minutes later to say he had just pronounced our son dead, I was prepared for that. While I faintly remember trying to ask the doctor what time Mac died, I suppose I realized the full impact of the shock then. If the doctor answered, I didn't comprehend. Strangely enough, my only real strong recollection or knowledge of passing time that whole evening was from that point at 6:19 until the doctor came in and told us Mac had died.

At some time after that, our minister and various family members began arriving at the hospital. Other neighbors, who are also dear friends, had brought our daughter, Heather. Eventually that night, I had to make the decision to notify a funeral director to care for Mac's body. I still can't understand how I was able to attend to details like that. But our family and our minister were there with us, and together we handled arrangements then and in the next few days, as well.

Finally, the nurse asked if we would like to go in and be with Mac for a few minutes, and I said that I would. I was doing everything in very slow motion — speaking slowly and moving slowly. I was aware of that, but couldn't adjust it. My sister walked in with me, and together we stood beside the table where Mac was lying.

I looked down at him and said, "You're not in there, are you, McCall?"

We stood there for a few minutes, and I bent down to kiss him. He didn't seem to be there. That's all I can say. It was the form of Mac, void of the rest of him. I very much felt his absence from his body. I don't know how else to describe it.

We went home, accompanied by family and several friends. After the back door was opened, I flipped the porch lights on. Only one lit up, and that one also burned out while everybody was entering the door. So, the first thing I did was go get a new light bulb and ask my brother to put it in the fixture. Our table was set, and the food was still on the stove. I said I wanted something to eat. What I wanted was a bite of the potatoes, because Mac had peeled them for me; I wanted to taste them for that reason. They gave me a whole plate full of food, thinking I wanted to eat because I was hungry, I guess. I did manage to take a taste of the potatoes! They were good . . . because Mac prepared them. One of our nieces stayed all night to be with Heather. I don't remember anything more after eating the potatoes. Everybody made sure we were settled for the night before they went home.

I have no recollection of whether we slept or not that night. All I recall is that I arose right before daylight and went out to sit on the back step. I was just beginning to break down, for the first time, when I remembered how happy Mac sounded. I thought, you sounded so full of joy, McCall! I'm going to try to be happy for you! I knew it wasn't going to be an easy thing — getting used to not having him here with me — but at least *I knew he was with God*. And whatever it was he was exclaiming about was more wonderful than words alone could describe. (He was always calling me to see something. It was as if he was saying, "You've got to see *this*, Mom! Boy, it's fabulous!")

Several weeks later, I began wondering why our neighbor Bill had responded as he did that night; why he looked so joyful. I thought, I wonder what *my face* looked like. Was that what made him look so happy? I returned some dishes to their house and spoke with his wife about what happened at the hospital. I said, "I'd like to tell you what Bill's face looked like when I turned toward him that night."

She said, "First, let me tell you what he said *your* face looked like." She proceeded to describe my face with the same glowing, beaming joy; joy that was evident within and without!

That was our gift; a gift that came in the midst of the worst moment of my life. It made all the difference in my ability to continue even wanting to live. After all, my Mac was fine. I just had to set about trying to be fine, too. Knowing that God had, through His Grace, given us a most wonderful gift, also made me think there was a reason *why* He allowed me to hear Mac entering the dimension beyond his life here.

It was months before we were emotionally capable of thinking about the accident. Although all of our family members and even our minister urged us to try when it was possible, we couldn't. They advised us that we would never be able to fully lay the experience to rest and go on with our lives unless we did. Finally, one day near the end of January, I decided that I could try; although, I didn't have any idea how to go about it. Eventually, I decided that since he left this life at the hospital, I'd begin there. I called and said I would like a report of all that happened in the emergency room the night of my son's accident. They said they would have the information for me the next day. When I arrived, they handed me an envelope and asked me to sign for it. I sat down in front of the desk to open it and read it right there. I figured if there were any questions about it, I'd be right there to have them answered.

The first page gave vital statistics of when they had admitted Mac. Then I flipped to the second page and saw a list of the exact *times*. Next to the list of times, they wrote everything they had done at that time. Hurriedly, I slid my finger down the list of times, looking for 6:19.

It said, *"6:20 — removed all CPR equipment."* The next pages were graphs of his heart beat. At 6:20 there was only a straight line, indicating his heart had stopped. I was *so happy* when I saw that! I sat there and laughed out loud and said, "Praise God!" When I tried to explain to the lady sitting at the desk that I *did* hear my son, I must have scared her! She got up and left.

I had never doubted, for one second, that I had heard Mac. Not even at my worst moments have I ever doubted that Mac was fine and with God. Most of the people close to us, with whom I had shared my experience, also received the account with great joy. But I wanted everyone else to know that *Mac was okay . . . more than okay.*

Loveshine

My son is in heaven . . .
yet as surely
As you greet
Your child each morning,
I send love to mine.
And, as obviously
As your son's bright smile
Shows he has heard you,
Loveshine's warmth
Enters my heart,
As well.

Kathryn Hardgrove Popio
Monday, January 6, 1989

2
A Place To Grieve

As Mac and I sat in the living room one morning of the summer before he left us, he looked around and said, "You know, we ought to call this the music room or the library instead of the living room. The piano and my trombone and music rack are here. And all the books are over there on the shelf. We hardly ever come in here just to sit. We read or play music. So, I think that's what we should call it!" I liked his suggestion, but we never really had time to put it into practice.

At the funeral, our minister advised us to choose a certain spot where we could go and be by ourselves and mourn. I automatically drifted into the "music room" every morning for that purpose. With three tall east windows, the morning sun poured in and made it a wonderously sunny place to think. Since that was where I used to station myself to see the kids off on the school bus every morning, I was already in the habit of being there early each day. After they'd leave for school, I would usually stay and pray. So, "the music room" became the place where I went every morning in my new situation to repeatedly seek God and to cry.

Before Mac left for school each morning that last spring, he had the habit of going to the piano and quickly running through the beginning of Scott Joplin's song, *The Entertainer*. Although he had played the violin before switching to the trombone, he loved to pick away at the piano, too. When I tried to persuade him to think of piano lessons, as well, he had said, "No offense, Mom, but I don't want to take piano lessons." So, I had only shown him correct finger placements on the piano keys, some scales, and a few elementary tunes. He enjoyed that much structure, and it enabled him to pick out a few songs that struck his fancy — like *The Entertainer*. He had been bound and determined to learn a portion of the basic melody that spring of 1988.

I'd point out the nuances Joplin employed as I went through the piece with him. After all, it was those nuances of the song that could wind his music through your senses. I considered those loud and soft places as important as the notes themselves.

Ah, but no . . .

Every morning while he waited for the school bus and every evening after supper, Mac's rendition went something like this:

"LA DAH, DAH, DAH! DAH DAH, DAH DAH-H-H!" as loud and as fast as he could make it strain itself and still be recognizable.

Then I'd play it again for him, pointing out the rich flavor of the man, himself, in addition to his music. Still, every morning and every evening Mac's version was:

"LA DAH, DAH, DAH! DAH DAH, DAH DAH-H-H!" until our entire household would clasp their hands over their ears, feeling fortunate he didn't know very much of it.

So, in those grief times that I became so familiar with, I would often glance over at the sheet music and be drawn to the piano where I'd play the first couple of measures with that same exhuberance and lack of credibility that Mac's versions always had. Once and a half through like that would usually cheer me up. When I finished, I'd see Mac smiling at me from the school photograph on the top of the piano, and I couldn't help but laugh a little about the sense of real fulfillment he got out of that song. Then I'd hold my thumb up in the air in a victory sign, get a Kleenex to blow my nose, and resume the business at hand — living the life left to me.

Going to the music room early each morning soon became one of my systems. I not only faced my grief every day, but I was also allowing myself the joy of an added little ritual of reviving some of the fun Mac had brought to me. It all worked together to express how much I missed my son and how neat I thought he was. We each need to find our own systems of releasing our feelings in order to recover. It's almost as simple as this: Whatever works at picking you up instead of pulling you down, *do that*!

Crying may very well be a healthy part of the system. It may be a part of your personal grieving system for a very long time. Tears are healing. Making the opportunity to express an appreciation for your loved one is also healing. In looking at the other philosophies people offer to halt your crying time — "try to pull yourself back together," and "don't let yourself think about him so much," — I simply say, you won't *succeed* in fooling yourself. Grieving is a task that must be accomplished.

It used to be my impression that when several months had passed after a funeral, mentioning the deceased would only bring up painful memories. I recall the time a friend's baby died, and I decided against going to see her because I didn't know what to say. Besides, I felt she'd "get over it" sooner if she was left to be consoled by her family. Now I know differently. After the funeral week, our family didn't come to visit unless invited; although, they were supportive in *many* other ways. They were trying to deal with the grief themselves and were in no shape to console us! This is quite typical about many grief situations. I often prayed for Mac's extended family and his friends while in the music room because I was aware that an overwhelming shock of this type would require many months to fully comprehend what had happened.

Mac's sister, Heather, refused to allow mourning into her day. She kept so busy with school and her friends, there was no time left. Therefore, it plagued her at night through varieties of dreams. These did not begin easing up until she was able to discuss them with me and analyze what they were telling her. In the book, *Helping Children Cope With Separation and Loss*, by Claudia Jewett, another helpful system of working through and finishing up the relationship with the deceased is proposed. The author suggests having the surviving person seat herself opposite an empty chair and begin calling things to mind she would liked to have said to her brother.

In eventually talking about her dreams, Heather related to me that she and Mac were just beginning to reach a more mature and close relationship as brother and sister that last summer. She expressed how glad she was that she could know that. She also found that her dreams were constantly saying what she refused to admit to herself — she missed her brother enormously. Heather said, "I was acting as if nothing unusual happened in my life because I was out in the world and was reacting to how they were treating me; which was no different." She confessed, "I never realized what an interesting person Mac was. I took his chatter for granted and mostly tried to tune him out." At that point, Heather and I were able to discuss the fact of that tendency being pretty normal for a brother and sister. Thus, Heather was finally able to do what I had also found needed to be done — verbally express an intense "homesickness" for her brother and also enjoy an appreciation for the person he was.

I can attest to how much these physical acts — that is, actually going through the motions or taking certain real steps — can create a sense of *completeness*; for they satisfy previously unmet needs of the unconscious mind. When our hurt is so enormous, specific areas of concern often cannot be singled out to focus on and deal with. We tend to think, "How would I ever begin? I'm not even going to try! Then it won't hurt so much! I'll just go about my life as usual and pretend it doesn't bother me! Yeah! That sounds like a good idea."

For example, it took almost a year for me to say out loud, "I miss you, Mac." I could silently pray about it to God. I could repeatedly write it in my journal, but I carefully kept myself from saying it out loud. Why? Because I didn't want Mac to hear me. I didn't want his joy to be diminished because I was so sad. (That's a mother's thinking.) Eventually, God allowed me to feel that Mac was very near to me and *knew* I missed him. When that realization dawned on me, I said it out loud, as if I were speaking directly to him. The flood of tears that followed was a relief. That small action seemed to settle something inside of me.

It has been my experience that taking time to *allow* feelings to flow exposes specific hurts, one by one. So, one by one, I confronted them, dealt with them, and began experiencing the healing I always anticipated. This may be an experience a surviving person can accomplish alone or it may help to have a trusted companion to supply encouragement. It should always be seen as an option and never forced. Through this process of establishing a tie to the friend who is gone, surprising conversations may be fulfilled.

Establishing your personal place to go and be alone also accommodates part of the need for a physical reality we have missed because of circumstances beyond our control. This *place* supplies a reality, of sorts, at a time when most of life seems like an unreality. No decision has to be made each time as to "where can I go to be by myself and think?" It was also the opportunity to open myself to God's comfort. Many times I felt God speaking to my inner heart, assuring me of Mac's well-being and making me feel the promise of my own recovery. A lot of healing went on in that "music room." And I cannot imagine that it could have come if I had not opened myself to it each day.

Another spot that became a place of solace was Mac's bedroom. From the first day after the accident when our home filled with family and friends who came to support us, we all drifted into Mac's room. Even after he left, it had a vitality that exhilarated us beyond the sadness. How could it not be exhilarating? He left his menagerie of sea pets behind! And one does not enter a room with a live alligator without some rush of excitement! He had talked of being a marine biologist during his last year and a half. Toward that goal, he had had a series of unusual pets. There had been, over the years, several land turtles, hermit crabs that supplied a topic for his Young Author's book in fifth grade, tropical fish, fiddler crabs, sea monkeys (which I still have not quite figured out), a blue gill he had caught in his uncle's pond the week before he left, and then there was Carl the Caiman — who was of the alligator species. Carl, who measured approximately fifteen inches, had been a part of our household for about six months. Mac had more or less tamed him enough so that we could be casual observers through the aquarium glass without causing an alligator stir. Thus, Carl provided a much-needed focal point that brought forth comforting discussions.

During those days between his death and the funeral, our family and friends walked into his room and experienced life going on through these creatures Mackie liked. The night after he came back from a camping trip with his cousin, when he had caught the blue gill with a piece of string and a blade of grass, he asked if he could leave the tank light on so he could watch it swim around. "It just looks so peaceful that I'd like to lay here and watch it for a while before I go to sleep," he had said. So, even after Mac had left, his fish tanks were bubbling, Carl was sunning himself or hiding in the half of a clay flowerpot under the water, and all his fish pets were swimming around as usual. It actually was peaceful. Of course, we had to make sure his sea pets were fed, too. So, we'd all find ourselves mingling in there and talking about Carl. It became an activity that still connected us with Mac; once again, I mention an activity that became important because it gave us an opportunity to talk about Mac. At the funeral dinner, his buddies also got a charge out of going to see Carl again. And they'd ask about him in the months to come. Of course, we not only had to remember to feed the pets, but we had to clean their tanks, too; which meant another regular activity.

When we look at what grieving is all about, we should remember that Jesus, Himself, wept when His friend Lazarus died. Some cultures accommodate the mourning process and look upon certain rituals as being very healthy. I have come to believe that avoiding mourning (or trying to avoid it) is what is unhealthy. Once again, I received great comfort from coming to God in this second special place of remembering my son and his life with me. On one occasion recalled in my journal, I left his room having the feeling of "victorious completion." From that session of prayer, I felt that God was speaking to my inner heart with this precise message: "He lives with me." The exhilaration of that experience is constantly vivid and uplifting and continued comforting me in another place where grieving must eventually be realized — the grave site.

Peter, Heather and I had gone there the evening of the day of his body's burial. But it was one week later before I went alone to the grave site. When I got out of the car, it looked like the farthest place in the world to walk to. Halfway there, I began crying. I walked over, sat down, and continued crying and thinking and missing him. Soon I noticed a woman approaching me. She spoke cautiously as she came closer, asking if I was all right. I said I was, and that this was the first time I had come by myself to visit the grave site. Then she came and stood by me and asked who it was that I had lost. I told her it was my son; that he had just turned thirteen and had been hit by a car. And she sat down beside me and started crying along with me. She said she had two sons who were grown and lived far away, so she didn't get to see them very often.

Then she asked what his name was, and I told her his name and mine. She said, "My name is Mary."

She stayed for another few minutes and then went to tend her husband's grave; which I later realized was quite a distance away. After she left, I felt more peaceful. By the time I left the cemetery that afternoon, it seemed as if I had had another gift of comfort supplied by my Lord — someone who came to grieve with me at a place that was extremely painful to face. He even supplied someone with the same name as His own mother; more expressions of His complete understanding and compassion for the loss I experienced and for the difficult task I had of trying to adjust to it.

On another occasion when I stood there, I felt as if the Holy Spirit was inwardly assuring me, "He's not here." Then I recalled the earlier message, "He lives with me." Those are the thoughts that prevail at every visit to the site since then.

These places became oasises, allowing me to exercise my feelings at my own pace. In these places, I received prescriptions and balms from my Lord that were especially *right for me*. And through the many months ahead, God fulfilled His promise when He assured His people saying, "I will not leave you comfortless."

Morning Returns

Morning still returns,
As it did when Macaulay was here,
Waking from the night rest;
As it did when warm showers
Sparkled over his body
And enthusiastic songs
Mingled with rising steam,
Baptizing him . . . and the bathroom.
Yes, the morning still returns,
And my heart roams the house,
Remembering.

Kathryn Hardgrove Popio
Wednesday, January 3, 1990
7:50 a.m.

3
Grief Peaks

When I've thought of things I have had to do to continue with my life and healing, I can't help but liken them with a scene from a Peter Falk movie our family has enjoyed called *The In-laws.* In one part, the two fathers are zooming down the highway in a small South American village on political espionage business and are being chased by two gunmen in a car behind them. Suddenly, they drive up behind a huge truck loaded with bananas. As part of the ploy to stop the car that has been shooting at them, Peter Falk aims his gun at the banana truck, shoots and then quickly passes the truck and escapes the tonnage of bananas that pours onto the highway. Of course, the chase car spins out of control and crashes. There have been many places I've gone since Mac left that were as threatening to me as that truckload of slippery bananas was to the pursuers in the movie; places that seemed to have this message: "If you come here, you'll be out of control, and it will be an awfully painful scene. So don't even try."

After a loss, grieving persons are confronted with numerous experiences and places that appear as insurmountable emotional mountains. The first of these "grief peaks" that scared me was the supermarket. It was chuck-full of lifelong associations with Mac. In the first weeks, just seeing juice boxes could cause a reaction because he drank those every day. That was something we *always* bought. Furthermore, Mac usually accompanied me to the market. He liked to cook, so he went to the market and helped select things for our menu that he would enjoy making. After his death, the idea of going there sounded like an impossibility. I found myself asking Heather, my daughter, to go pick up a few things. That went on for several weeks. I have a friend whose little boy, Peter, died of cancer at a young age. Even seeing a grocery cart was enough to set her off in a flood of painful memories because Peter used to ride in the cart. The empty cart felt unnatural. Therefore, grocery shopping was a painful experience from the minute she arrived at the store. It's one of the things you have to learn to overcome.

In my case, this process began by confessing to my close friend that the thought of going to the supermarket scared me so much that I didn't know if I could ever go back. We were returning from a drive one Saturday afternoon; we had gone to lunch and a drive in Amish Country for a few hours. One might suppose if I could go to lunch in a restaurant, I could go to the supermarket. *Wrong*! While the restaurant was one where I had taken Mac and Heather before, it wasn't part of our weekly routine. Grocery shopping was.

My friend said, "Do you want to stop there on the way home today?"

This was similar to asking me if I wanted to drive in the Indianapolis 500! The thought of being back in our supermarket that afternoon — in an hour or so — took my breath away! I can still feel the pressure caused by my fear that day.

I laughed at first, embarrassed that I needed someone to act like a babysitter; for that's what it seemed like; she'd be walking along with me, emotionally holding my hand. I told her that's how it felt. She just said, "Well, if you want me to go with you, I will. But if you want to wait until another day, that will be okay, too. I'll go with you when you feel ready." Without either of us realizing it, she was setting a precedent I would be following in the future. She wasn't forcing me to accept her help. She offered, and it was my decision.

I said, "Yes. I would like for you to go with me." I suppose I agreed to try mainly because I envisioned the alternative — being forced to go some day all alone. Afterward, I congratulated myself for being smart enough to realize that I did, indeed, need a buddy with me to embark on such an emotionally-packed scene for the first time. I said, "I'll just pick up a few things and not try to do all the shopping. I think I can do that. And I want to do it."

Before we went into the store, she told me that if I felt at any time like leaving immediately, we would. She said, "Don't worry about leaving your cart and going back to the car. I'll handle the groceries in that case." Once again, I felt very free in this whole enterprise. (She helped me so perfectly.) Luckily, we went to the market at a rather slow time in the day. That's another good thing to plan for in a case like this. I was to find out later that many things could be faced if I'd set up realistic expectations for myself and do some preplanning. I was also fortunate that I didn't run into anybody I knew, because *that* would have been another difficult experience.

So, there we were, walking across the parking lot with as much trepidation as if we were approaching a picket line. We took two carts, even though we were together. That way, I would feel somewhat as if I were on my own. We walked very slowly, and she assured me once again that if at any time I wanted to leave, we could do so. I purchased a small supply for the week ahead, and so did she. I saw the food that I might ordinarily buy for Mac, and I *thoughtfully* passed it by. At the check-out counter, more memories confronted me. Mac used to help me unload the food items, and it wouldn't be unusual to see something I wouldn't have selected in a blue moon move along the automatic conveyor belt toward the UPC computer. That was when I'd narrow my eyes at him, and he'd usually shrug and say, "I just wanted to try that once." Then we'd glare at each other for a few seconds and decide between us if it was reasonable or whether we should put it back. It was one of those weekly games mothers and kids play, I suppose. Hundreds of shopping experiences would have to be let loose eventually. I could see that. It was going to be painful. But, Mac would want me to try to keep facing life. Yeah, I knew that, too. I felt really proud of myself as we left the market; proud of myself and glad to have such a dear friend who would fill in as one of God's angels, actually. Together, we had taken the first of many difficult steps. One milestone down and many to go.

Sometime in the beginning of the grief process, we need to acknowledge that we are burdened by a tremendous sorrow. It's like identifying a foe. After admitting that the supermarket scared me, I then had to open up to strategies for handling it. I was fortunate enough to be surrounded by people who were not only willing to lend me their support, but were very capable, sensitive and persistent. Since I always felt that God had allowed His gift of assurance to enable a fine healing — healing that would allow me to eventually resume an enthusiasm for life — I accepted each and every person who reached out to me. There have been many hands with a variety of healing gifts put at my disposal, and I continually thank God for them all. One by one, I decided to deal with my "grief peaks" until they became, at least, easier.

There is no getting around pain forever. It has to be met and dealt with or it stays a strong force inside. In the early days of mourning, it was a steady companion. There was no getting around fear, either. I believe this is true whether the loss you had was sudden or gradually came into your life. Even in those early weeks, however, I felt I needed to participate in the world to some degree or I would not be doing myself any kindness. I chose to do myself the favor of transforming my grief peaks back into places of casual encounters. I am ever thankful that I could try.

If there is anything I would stress to people trying to help in situations of grief, it would be this: Be there, be gentle and appropriately persistent. That means, employing some intuition about how the person seems to be handling the various steps of getting on in his/her life. A storm-trooper approach could do more harm than good. In fact, it could do permanent damage and undermine the chances of attempting again at a later time. I am thankful that I was surrounded by understanding friends to help me succeed in wanting to try to recover from my grief. I almost feel like putting that last statement in bronze. Without them, I wouldn't be as far as I am in the healing process. Also, without knowing Mac was okay, I don't think I would have been able to move along even with all the help I got.

There are numerous moves that people going through the grief process cannot seem to force themselves to make. Even more frustrating, I couldn't explain why! Why, for example, should a person be encompassed with so much anxiety that she couldn't even go to the supermarket by herself? I had spoken in front of large groups of strangers prior to Mac's absence; yet, there I was, afraid to go to any number of places. They were places so full of memories that the very thought of them seemed to scream, "There's a lot of pain here!" And my emotions were so raw, I couldn't dare add any more weight to what I was already carrying.

Somebody I shared this with said that when her brother had died, she actually walked several blocks out of her way to work every day to avoid going past a store that held a lot of memories for her. I didn't put undo pressure on myself to face those zenith grief sites in my life. However, I did try to look at them one at a time; in that individualized way, I could better determine if I felt ready to neutralize those pain-filled places. It may be possible to take one step and one step and one step along towards the difficult things to face. It's a matter of sensing our own readiness.

In another instance, a friend of mine went with me to sit in the park in our community one afternoon to help me to desensitize myself to that area where a family wedding was to take place in the coming weeks. It was filled with so many memories of my life with Mac that I thought there was no way I could attend that wedding. After all, weddings are emotional times in themselves, without adding grief that Mac wouldn't be there to be a part of it with us. Furthermore, Mac's close friend lived right across the street from the park.

I wanted to go to the wedding. But could I? Well, my friend and I packed our lunches and sat on the park bench for more than two hours. We talked about everything under the sun; anything we wanted to discuss, we did. Finally, I looked at her and said, "Well, with just you and me here, I feel fine. But I don't know if it will work the day of the wedding."

Once again, however, I remembered the "supermarket attitude." If I felt overwhelmed when I got there, I could leave. Nobody was going to chain me down, after all. It was, once again, my own decision.

I decided to try to go. It was frightening. Yes. But, I succeeded. Again. And I was happy that I tried. Someone later offered this insight: When I went ahead of time to sit in the park and chat, I further neutralized the painful memories by creating a pleasant new one on top of them. I suppose this could be likened to putting a blanket on a cement step before sitting on it on a cold day. It does make a difference in the experience.

Stepping With Time

It's not Time that brings relief
From sadness and problems,
It's how you spend Time,
How you train your frame of mind.
It's Faith that something is possible
To be built in place of rubble;
Faith that God's Infinite Plan
Is too marvelous to topple
By my human misfortune.

Kathryn Hardgrove Popio
December 31, 1989
(Late at night)

4
Doing The Next Thing
Again And Again

Losing a loved-one unexpectedly — in an instant — is not easy to comprehend. It is even more difficult to understand when you feel he went much sooner than he should have. Mark Twain described it so well when he said, "It is one of the great mysteries of our nature that a man all unprepared can receive a thunder stroke like that (death of his daughter, Suzy) and live."

Eventually in the aftermath of your loss, some people will say, "You have to go on with your life." They will, undoubtedly, not be people well-acquainted with the process of grieving. If they were, they would have, instead, supported my struggle toward wanting to say that for myself. They would have understood it takes a lot of time for the overpowering pain to ease up enough to even *want* to go on with life, much less initiate steps to do it.

I feel very deeply that we must try with all we've got in our reserve of spirit and mind to comprehend what happened to us. Trying to deny the tremendous grief that engulfs every waking hour will only result in a preservation and recreation of the pain at some future date. Shutting the doors on mourning too early may not enable us to reach that state of fine healing where a healthy outlook returns.

While I can't stress enough the medicinal benefit of the freedom to express sadness, observations, concerns and fears, I also cannot stress enough the comfort and assurance derived from knowing I had freedom to chart my own course of recovery from my grieving state, as well. After about nine months of mourning, I saw this quote from Rose Fitzgerald Kennedy, mother of John F. Kennedy:

"Birds sing after a storm;
Why shouldn't people feel as free
To delight in whatever remains to them?"

When I first read that, I had just experienced two whole days without tears, and her words sounded refreshing to me. Here was someone else who had lost children and decided to relish life again! I was ready to want that a little, myself.

During the earliest days of grief, my belief in God's gift of life beyond this one has comforted me. Eternal life is the ultimate extension of our lives here. As time has moved along, my belief has continually given me reason to fight the terrible handicap called grief. Of course, it meant facing days that defied me to be happy. I rose to the challenge, however, because I felt that allowing myself to label certain dates as sad for all future time would be denying the richness that Mac and others have given me. To wage such an enormous battle, mourning parents must, in the end, find a way of realizing the firm eternal existence and value of their loved-one's life. This is quite necessary for restoring an outlook that's healthy enough to attend to an appreciation of their own life . . . for getting onto the paved highway and off the rutted, bumpy road of grief.

The bereaved parent has to set the precedents. To me, this means acknowledging the vitality of your loved-one's life in the very core of your being. They existed and are valuable; no matter how long or short that life was. It is extremely essential to record his or her contribution to the richness you now carry with you into the future.

This note in my journal proves that, while such a task is hard because we are dealing with an intangible — love, the hard task may see victory:

February 8, 1989

I feel almost normal this morning; not that I had no thought of Mac. But I feel as though our relationship is **there** *(like Heather's and mine) and God is reigning supreme in our lives and is also* **there** *for us. What's different about that then any other time? It's a* **reality** *of* **wellness** *. . . it's a kind of* **knowing***.*

K.P.

About six months after I first realized this state of *knowing*, several friends told me I was starting to seem like my old self again. Even though a lot came between, it was another example of the journal illuminating my inner feelings so that I could reevaluate them later. Results of what I was beginning to focus on and strive for eventually became apparent to others.

In writing, that sounds so assured and simple . . . do this and you'll reach your satisfying "new normal" in life . . . do that and you'll feel less pain.

"Tra-la-la."

I would be the last one to say there's anything simple about striving to resume life after losing a large portion of the whole reason for trying in the first place. It's hard work, and it's work that constantly meets a resistive heart. I certainly saw contradiction in that goal for myself; times when facing the new day carried a weight so heavy I couldn't see anything else except my loss. It was like getting up each day and trying to function with a grand piano tied to my body and mind! For

41

when a bereaved person says, "I just can't make myself feel like trying," it is quite a different matter than it is for a person who is not grieving.

Sometimes people would say, "Oh, I've felt like that lots of times," and they'd more or less shrug off my lament. I didn't say this out loud, of course, but there were times when I looked at people like that and secretly shouted, "No, you probably never have felt *just like this*, or you wouldn't be so quick to subtract from what I have just said."

Of course, everybody has had stress-filled, depressed, non-productive days. But they don't begin to fall into the same category. Not even the sudden death of my mother, whom I was also extremely close to all my life, fell into this category. I'm sure you would join me in saying this next sentence to all those unknowing persons who say they know how bereaved parents must feel: "Nobody knows unless they have experienced it."

None of the near misses people share to relate to your pain even come close to true empathy! And when it comes right down to it, would I wish knowledge of that kind of pain on someone else? Of course not. But we can share encouragement with one another, and we can share strengths for coping with one another.

I sought such strengths as I reached for healing, and I came across insights from others whose lives spanned many decades. They were from people who had once known that same piano weight I was experiencing; that same enormous burden encompassed by the word "grief." Their thoughts, found here and there, were soothing to my spirit and often encouraged my willingness to keep trying. They were acknowledging concrete emotions and reminding me that I was experiencing a very human condition that many others had known — human heartache. I could identify with them, and from across the ages I felt a keen sense of timeless humanity uplifting me.

For example, there was a journalist named Adela Rogers St. John whom I always admired from the Merv Griffin television show days because, even in her elderly years, she emitted a rich enthusiasm for life. Later, I learned she had lost a son through the war. Her advice on coping was this: "Do ye now next thing." It sounded like a line from a Shakespearian play. I don't know where she first heard it and decided to adapt it to her circumstances, but I considered its value and took it as my own motto. I have repeated that to myself hundreds of times; times when I'd stand in a daze and mutter, "I just *can't* get myself going. *I can't.*" That little phrase would come to mind along with the realization that action breeds more action, and I would set about doing *something*; even if it wasn't very much.

I don't want to make that philosophy sound overly simple. It's not simple to pull yourself up when every part of you feels like staying slumped in a chair crying. I am just saying, after you cry awhile, *try* to get up and *do the next thing*. It may be dishes. It may be getting dressed for the day. Or, there were days when my one major accomplishment was to make sure the coffee pot was clean and ready for use in case company came. It might be getting out an inspirational book that has potential for reviving a sagging spirit. Whether the task I did was large or very small, I patted myself on the back for getting up and making the attempt on some of those down (way down) days.

The last birthday gift Mac gave me was a bottle of Jasmine spray cologne. After he left, I'd open the medicine cabinet and spray that on when I was trying to pull myself together to go out somewhere. Breathing the fragrance gave me a real lift. I had also placed one of his prettiest hermit crab shells on my make-up tray some time during that first year because it brought thoughts of happy times. They supplied an extra push by reminding me that Mac was most likely rooting for me to enjoy further blessings in my life.

Those little incentives, noticeably effective in planting seeds of love to replace emptiness, began to expand when one day I came across a small framed photo of Jesus that the kids had gotten in Sunday School when they were very small. While its miniscule size didn't lend itself to being very noticeable in the rest of the house, it was perfect to set on the medicine cabinet shelves to look at when I opened it for deodorant and perfume in the morning. Seeing the peaceful, loving face of Jesus made me feel warm and thankful. Within an instant, the promise His life brought to dreary reality revived my outlook; which was a considerable plus to count on as I began trying to do the next thing day after day after day.

Gradually, I added other bits of this special "medicine;" keepsakes that one might otherwise discard, I'd appropriate for my medicine cabinet. Short inspirational articles that supplied extra encouragement when I was down were things I placed in various spots around the house. So of course, I put a few in my medicine cabinet.

Leafing through Mac's photo album, I saw a snapshot of that same hermit crab I had on my tray beside the sink, taken when it was alive with activity. So I put that in a tiny plastic frame on another shelf. Looking at the reality of the shell and the memory of that seemingly inanimate object moving about on the patio that day (I don't remember what Mac called that particular hermit crab), served to remind me that the reverse is true for humans. Whereas our shells stay behind to deteriorate, the essence of what is truly *us* goes on to newness of life. But, long after the sea crab is deceased, the reality of its existence is preserved for years to come through its enamel-like shell.

Eventually, I began running out of Jasmine spray. But by that time, I still had the other pick-me-uppers. Besides, I have to laugh that I would have hated hermit crabs and been afraid of them if it weren't for Mac. I was a fluffy dog and cat person all my life. If anyone predicted I would be playing with hermit crabs and talking to an alligator that lived in my house, I would have said they were talking craziness. Mac's interests brought a much broader outlook to many aspects of creation. And I still rejoice in the enthusiasm for sea life I have inherited from my son.

Enthusiasm is a rare commodity for a bereaved person. It must be purposefully sought and nurtured for the gem it is.

When one of my dearest friends was recovering from cancer, she planned something to look forward to on those days when she predicted she'd have more strength. Those events became like solar power to her spirit during the other days she had to endure, so she advised me to do the same thing when I lost Mac; to write things on the calendar to look forward to. I have found that to be wise advice. Knowing you have something pleasant to do tomorrow (and next week) invigorates your spirit; just like those mental pats on the back you give yourself for trying to move along each day do. My advice then would be, don't be sparing with either of them. Striving to recover and build a satisfying "new normal" is reason to be proud of yourself. I have found that *gently* pushing for this recovery gives me a more pleasant countenance that also makes it easier for others to be around me. And that utimately boosts my spirit, too.

I remember a line from a Disney movie the kids and I saw. It was called *The Richest Cat In The World*, and Mac taped it because he enjoyed it so much. The main character, a cat who could talk to just a few people, was trying to convince a human friend to take a more realistic attitude about the goal they were pursuing. Thus, Leo the cat gave this advice: "Inch by inch, life's a cinch. Yard by yard, it's very hard." That's the way to begin . . . an inch at a time. After all, an inch is enough of a challenge to someone who is mourning and won't have a firm commitment to life for quite some time.

A Red Tulip At Dawn

New red tulip
Tall and lush,
Once pointing
At the dawn,
Now hand-delivered
As an afterthought
By my school-bound son.
Offered with gallant flair
In early morning . . .
New tulip freshness,
New tulip softly fragrant
Against my lips and cheek;
Fragile long-stemmed
Launcher of dreams.

Kathryn Hardgrove Popio
Wednesday, April 27, 1988
6:45 a.m.

5
A Time For Putting Away

Carl, the alligator, watched as we survived the week of Mac's funeral. Strange as it sounds, he provided a lively focus for all the family. Nobody could go into Mac's room and totally concentrate on sadness because Carl was there in his aquarium; watching you. Every one of us eventually wound up sitting on Mac's bed watching Carl and the other sea creatures swimming in bliss. It seemed so normal there! His room was vital and peaceful. It was appropriate because their owner was also vital.

Since Carl's supply of goldfish dinners had dwindled by the following week, we had to take care of that. We couldn't have a hungry alligator on our hands. Soon after, we knew his home also had to be cleaned to get rid of the green algae buildup. I tried to mop the glass sides with a sponge-tipped stick; which noticeably perturbed Carl. He hadn't had any personal handling (believe me) since his owner left, and he did not like the new faces he was seeing around his tank. When I noticed the algae had spread to his head, guilt also began creeping up on me. That was what prompted me to try to wipe his head with the sponge, and he let me know he really didn't care for that. It wasn't long before I realized Carl's needs were beyond our ability to handle them. Nobody else in the family had that much courage or confidence in Carl's friendly side. Therefore, as the weeks progressed, whenever anyone would ask how Carl was doing, I'd mention that we were trying to find a good home for him. In another month or so we had several offers.

Deciding whom he would be happiest with involved consideration for the welfare of the adopted family, as well. While there were several children who had an eye for this type of pet, we were also looking for someone who had knowledge or experience with exotic pets. In the end, we leaned toward a friend who had majored in biology in college and had actually spent some time in Africa during her studies. It was quite a relief to know that Carl would be going to someone who felt quite confident to put up with his special needs. The week before Mac left, this same friend had been at our home observing some of his creatures. And Mac, himself, had been noticeably impressed with her expertise. So, I'm sure he would have approved of our turning Carl over to her.

Of course, we couldn't let Carl leave with a dirty aquarium. But in the process of cleaning Carl and his surroundings, we antagonized him to the point of fearing he would try to escape; which he almost did. Before we were through, we had aquarium water all over the braided rug so that we also had to roll that up and put it outside to dry. All this led to the pleasant afternoon when his new family pulled up in the driveway to claim him — lock, stock and aquarium. So, that was the very first change we made within our household; once again, we did it with Carl's assistance. Yet when he left, he did not look back and neither did we.

I know many well-meaning people believe that cleaning out the deceased's belongings immediately after the funeral is a good idea. I did not find that to be true. Even if the child was an infant who was never even brought home to use the bedroom, I believe parents need to allow time to exprience the place that was prepared for their baby; the one place in the world which belonged to the child. Used or unused, it also serves to verify that the child existed, and that you loved the child enough to ready their special place. In so doing, you are, once again, allowing your feelings to find expression. You are also opening yourself to God's avenues of providing significant, quite personal ways to bring healing to you.

I made this note in my journal a month after Mac left:

Wednesday, September 21, 1988
In the beginning, I told myself I'd clear his things away before the holidays. Everybody said that sounded like a positive move. Then, after he had been gone for three-plus weeks, I felt as if the comfort of seeing his belongings in there (fish tanks bubbling and dresser arranged with his hair brush and styling gel) was something I HAD to keep in motion; for it all worked together to say, "Yes, you had a son."

In clearing everything away, I would have been eliminating another means of working through my grief. I was quickly realizing out of sight was never going to be out of mind. After the possessions are gone, it occasionally seems no one else realizes your child existed. And that is painful, too. When an older person dies, others may be more open to mentioning them; whereas, in the case of a child, even those close to you seem to feel that if they don't mention the child, your pain will diminish. They don't realize that their silence seems to deny you even had a loss. I think that is one of the differences about losing a child. Bereaved parents need their loved-one mentioned, too. A friend of mine who lost her adult son, Eric, said the lack of tangible reminders increased her sense of loss when she moved to another state; particularly, because those new friends never knew anything about her son. Thus, she felt the emptiness of loss all the more.

Possibly because children have had limited opportunity to make their mark in the world or have a long history (I'm still not sure myself), the parents may find themselves unusually diligent about preserving signs of their existence. For example, I remember giving a lot of thought to throwing away the empty peanut butter jar after Mac left because it was the last one I bought for my son. Something that anyone else would view as trash, I held as a memento.

When I cleaned out the cupboards the following year, I wrestled with the idea of throwing away the newspaper shelving that preserved the date when my family was intact. I remember when the last of the hair mousse was used from Mac's bottle, and I let it sit there empty (and even drew a picture of that in my journal) to recall when Mac began taming his teenage hair. When I confessed it to Heather, she simply said, "What are you hurting by keeping it a while longer?" Such simple logic; such truth there. What was I hurting? As long as it served a purpose, I kept it. The purpose it served was to help prove that my son existed. When you've lost a child, that becomes a very grand purpose!

In my case, one by one over the months and years, I have been able to release some of those mementos. After a year and a half, I washed his fingerprints off our wall behind the couch. Still, when Pete repapered the walls, and I moved my office into Mac's room, we left the ceiling just as it had been when Mac was here. I can still look up and see marks from a suction cup that hit the ceiling and fingerprints where he apparently got up on a chair to pull it down. I keep them there because it seems that's the way it should be. Ever so gradually and thoughtfully, I feel *ready* to part with some of those "less worthy" tangible reminders.

In our hurry-up society, we still come upon some things that cannot be hurried. Since God provided parents with nine whole months to get used to having a child, it is not unreasonable to believe that it will take at least that long to get used to their child's absence again from your lives. In carrying an infant in your womb for nearly a year, I can't help but feel there is *some* history, even in that short time, that can be realized, absorbed and celebrated.

Because Mac's spirit was extremely vital, even when his body and mind were pronounced dead, I have the confidence to believe that whether your child lived an hour or 4,760 days like McCall did, she or he was a part of your life. They were a living part of you that you lost. When we come to God and acknowledge our pain, I feel He has a special way of comforting each of us parents, brothers and sisters, grandparents, aunts and uncles and friends; that is, if we permit Him to do so by opening ourselves to that comfort and release of our grief.

Releasing our grief is what it is all about in the months ahead. How can we claim God's promise when He has said in John 14:18, "I will not leave you comfortless," if we try to walk away and pretend we don't need comforting? In allowing myself the opportunities to internalize everything I could about the times we shared with Macaulay and fully absorb every possible ounce of the richness of the love that existed between us, I felt more content about moving on. It also illuminated another promise of God's reality; that is, love survives.

In those grieving places I mentioned earlier (and many others besides), I asked for comfort. Over and over, I asked. And over and over the first couple of years, I received comfort that could only be brought through a loving God. For that whole first year, Mac's sister and I went into his room and sat to let his earthly possessions remind us of the time he spent with us. I was not devoid of future plans for the room — that was where I would set up an office for myself; replacing the tiny space I had in the basement. Ever so gradually, I let myself think of where I'd put my desk and how I'd arrange things. Ever so gradually, I was letting go of the past and trying to search for what the future would unfold for me. When I would mention having an office in Mac's room, people looked a little concerned that I could concentrate in there; they were probably basically concerned that it would hold too many bad memories. On the contrary, it held only the best memories. And in all those days that I sat and absorbed as many memories as I could, it truly became a place of comfort and healing.

I had gone to a craft show with my sister-in-law and niece that first fall and purchased a framed motto to hang on the wall. That served as my down-payment on using Mac's room as office space. It just took longer to take his things down and hang those of my own choosing than I realized. One of my friends who had lost a child many years earlier said that when the time for putting his things away was right, I'd know it. So, I waited for that time; for the time when everything in my heart and mind said, "Now."

The following year, when school started another time without Mac, and he didn't get off the school bus with the others, I went to his room and took down his Pee-Wee Herman poster hanging on the bedroom door. Then I sat down and cried. That was all I could handle that day, but I did realize the time had come. The pain of keeping his room intact, of watching dust collect and no new vitality promised the way it was, *outweighed* the comfort of seeing his belongings each day. Mac was so lively that it was seeming like more and more of a shame to let everything sit and gather dust. I was positive that life had to move on, even in that room; or *especially* in that room.

The next day I took down two other posters and sat and cried some more. The third day, I moved along, packing and remembering and putting away. Eventually, I got caught up in what I would be giving to his buddies and to his family. I wanted the things to be very specially placed. And so I attended to that. By and by, I was thinking of choosing wallpaper that would befit an office. His room had always been a nursery or child's room. But that was the past.

Many times I have remembered something Mac said to me one day several weeks before he left. It came up, I believe, because I have delved into our family's history a lot and would mention it frequently to Heather and Mac. We were driving home from his performance with the Honors Band at the Medina County Fair when he looked over at me and said, "You like to think about the past a lot, don't you." (It wasn't a question, but more of a statement of observation.)

52

I said, "Well, yeah. Sometimes you can learn a lot by looking at the past."

To my logic, he simply replied, "I like to think about *now*."

Of course, I continued driving along home thinking, well, someday, McCall, you'll see what I mean. As it turned out, *I never forgot what he meant*. It turned out to be, in the end, another lesson from a child.

My McCall loved life better than just about anyone I have ever known before. So, I decided to try to take some of that advice, that attitude, for myself and see what I could do with it.

Nobody said it's easy. It's not easy . . . but it's possible.

Child's Play

A child's heart
Took me
By the hand,
And flipped
The hourglass
Of sand . . .
Lifting
My spirit
To its knoll;
Exposing cobwebs
Of my soul.

Kathryn Hardgrove Popio
copyright 1985

6
Being Your Own Good Friend

In the aftermath of focusing on your grief, there is this grand decision to be made: Do I want to be healed?

A friend of mine had a growth inside a bone in her foot for some time before seeing a doctor about it. When asked about the length of time she put up with it before deciding to investigate she said, "I just learned to compensate for it by walking on the side of my foot. Then it didn't hurt so much." As bereaved people, we may deal with our pain as my friend did with her foot; for that is one way. But perhaps we have some other choices to explore.

I remember that Jesus asked several people if they wanted to be healed before performing a miracle to rid them of their handicap. It sounds like a strange question at first. We'd immediately answer, "*Of course* I want to be healed." But, in reality, that means giving up our handicaps. Grief is a whole current of handicaps that move along through our days with us. Unless we stop at some point and sternly face them and call them by name, we may get used to their subtle pull on our lives and adjust to them.

Keeping a journal not only helped me become aware of milestones in my mourning journey, but it also helped highlight some handicaps I wasn't recognizing. Here are some notes I made to myself:

10:00 a.m.
Tuesday, December 20, 1988

He won't be back — ever. And I know that. I know that so well. And I've got to praise God for him and all I came to know through his life and his love, and I've got to decidedly move on in life as far as I am supposed to go. I'll never accomplish a thing by refusing to move on without Mac.

K.P.

9:15 a.m.
Thursday, December 22, 1988

Whatever the formula to get him back . . . I'd do it. In my own selfish need to see him again, I'd request it.

K.P.

3:05 p.m.
Monday, December 26, 1988

I was grieving very intensely in Mac's bedroom today. Then I began going through a pile of statements and bulletins on the dresser and glanced through one of the mourning booklets Roberta's church sent to us. One part said, "Heavenly Father, as you have sealed me to live under you in your kingdom so also strengthen me to surrender the loss of my loved one into your keeping. In Jesus name I pray. Amen."

(To Everything There is a Season:
For the Bereaved Christian
By Paul Keller)

I can't say I've remembered that lately; because I'd like to reclaim him. How can I do both? How can I surrender and still want the one I've surrendered back again? I can't do both. I see that. I'm faced with that knowledge.

Kathryn

So I came upon one of the hurdles my heart had been having difficulty with ever since Mac left . . . surrendering him to God . . . unqualifiedly.

Scarey.

Overwhelming.

Yet I knew I couldn't get on a clear track if I was headed in two directions at once. That's a very basic concept that I hadn't applied to my situation before.

There I was, at the end of my journal as well as at a crossroads (one of the first) in accepting my loss and moving on. What a task! How does one attempt that?

Something that I recognize as The Holy Spirit has always made sure I think of Mac in a vital way. It's not just a whimsical ideology of picturing your loved-one sitting on a cloud or having sprouted wings. I accept the fact that I do not understand *how* he exists today, only that *he does*. Yet that has made all the difference in my attitude about healing and seeking God's future plan for me in this here and now existence I face without Mac. Like many parents who have lost a child, I still wonder how he's doing and what he's doing. Heather said to me one day, "I can't believe you still wonder if Mac is behaving himself!" Yes, I wonder that. I'm his mother! Since I fully believe he exists somewhere, I still want the best for him. I still love him.

There's a story that supposedly my great-grandmother passed down about her childhood in Germany. She said that one day the owner of the land where they lived and worked came and said they wanted her sister for their own child. So, they took her to their fine house to live and didn't allow her to visit her family after that. However, my great-grandmother's mother used to wait near the fence by the owner's house until her daugher came into sight. Then she'd pass bowls of various foods, like sour cream, over to her, to make sure she had enough of the foods she should have. That was a prime example of someone saying to her, "You're not her mother any more," and the mother in her kept right on thinking like a mother, regardless.

This leads me to another very critical long-term issue that parents who have lost a child face: How do I comment on his absence from our family life from now on? I recently met a lady who is now a great-grandmother. Yet when someone asked her how many children she had, she answered like this:

"I raised seven children, but I had three others that I lost when they died as infants."

When I heard that openness of attitude, one totally void of any kind of denial about the facts, I couldn't help admire her freedom.

Some people feel, "Well, I don't want to depress other people. So I just mention the children that are alive."

Another said, "If I'm with people I don't know well, I tell them I have four children and leave it at that. But afterwards, something inside me cries out, 'No, I have *five* children.' It happens every time, even after all these years."

After Mac died, I found myself sitting and burning inside — probably literally turning bright red from the rush of pressure — when I'd be in a situation where I had to tell about myself. In the earliest time, I froze for a second and then blurted out something about myself that had little to do with anything personal. And I can also remember thinking, this is the last time I'm going to go to one of these functions where they might ask me something about my family. Well, that could really limit future social activity for myself.

Instead, I made a point of determining just what my philosophy on this whole issue was going to be in order to decide what to say in times where I was called upon to mention my immediate family members. (It's amazing the many guises these times can take — doctor's forms to fill out, church groups, casual meetings with old friends who may not know about your present life, jury duty, college classroom settings, job interviews.)

Because God allowed Mac to communicate with me as he left this life and entered his new existence, and he referred to me as "Mom" rather than "hey you," I decided there should be no hesitancy in assuming I still have a son. After all, some people have children who live in other countries and seldom ever hear from them, but they still acknowledge them as part of their family. A friend who lost twin infant daughters, Colleen and Caroline, agreed that was a strong issue to deal with. She said, "After three months, nobody thinks you should *ever* mention them again!"

After making this decision, I had the opportunity to test it during several social gatherings, and it worked quite well. As long as I was sure I had a son and a daughter, it didn't matter to anyone else what our relationship encompassed from here on out. And I still speak of instances from both of their childhoods, or from my pregnancies, as naturally as any mother does.

Also, because I know he is alive with God, I ask God to tell him that I love him every day. I believe God can do that. I believe God is an extremely loving God who *might* give such a message to my son. After all, his own son died, too. That was agony for Him. HE UNDERSTANDS HOW I FEEL. How wonderful it is to know that *somebody* really knows how I feel and how you feel.

Allowing myself the luxury of asking God to tell Mac I love him each day helps me heal. It also helps me continue, in some small way, that one particularly happy routine of my life — that is, of telling Macaulay I love him. It's always followed by that clear recall of hearing him answer with, "I love you, too, Mom." I am nourished and refreshed by feelings of a love that is not totally lost, but is still flowing. I am *not* telling myself I will be seeing Mac on the weekend. I am *not* telling myself he's away at college and will be returning to Ohio soon. However, just as a mother with a child across the country knows her child still exists, even though she can't see him everyday any more, feels free to mention him/her with love, so I accept that freedom, as well. Why should we lose all privileges of *speaking* of our child in a normal way in addition to losing them physically?

Abraham Maslow said in his book, *The Farther Reaches of Human Nature*:

*"The past is active and alive
only insofar as it has
recreated the person,
and has been digested
into the present person."*

When I read that, I realized even more fully, that the way I have met mourning — head on — has permitted a digestion of the past. Avoiding your grief and pretending you are as normal as anybody else in the work-a-day world is not being your own friend. Grief has a way of resurfacing when you least expect it. I guess we could say that is one of *grief's norms*, regardless of who you are or where you travel to escape it.

My efforts to permit grief have brought many more rewards than I could ever imagine. Otherwise, it's like going out in a blizzard and telling myself it's just like any other day. My mind may be very determined, but pretty soon my body is going to rebel and fall along the wayside. Denial, emotional distractions and ignoring my handicaps will only hinder the job at hand — that is, creating an opportunity for a fine healing.

Acknowledging my grief has allowed me to chart my own course for moving forward. Still, that course has always been facilitated by my family and friends. While participating in a workshop on grief support, I heard many people confess that they stayed away from some grief situations because they didn't know what to say. One of our biggest human errors comes from thinking we should (and may) say the right things in all situations.

The best attitude for all — the bereaved as well as their supporters — is to realize no one is capable of saying the perfect thing in all circumstances. Those people who feel they have the capacity of summarizing God's insight might help more by listening. Listening is highly underrated! I have seen *God* do marvelous things through people who were just willing to be there and listen. Sometimes, the perfect helpers are the ones who admit, "I don't know what you are feeling. But I care and will try to help you keep going."

I have a friend and a niece who both live in other states, but made a point to call or send a card at regular intervals so I could count on some pick-me-upper to keep coming during that first year or so. And I am so thankful my friends never hesitated to invite me to lunch, or just give me a hug and say, "I'm remembering you in prayer." I have found that I continue calling those beautiful gestures to memory and thanking God for such blessings many times throughout the year, so they have never ceased in bringing fresh joy every time I think of them. All these things have been an important ingredient in my healing.

People are one of God's vital avenues for bringing us comfort. If I would have shut myself off from people, I would have been stiffling opportunities for healing. I've tried never to allow myself to do that. Sometimes I've had to tell people who offered invitations for this or that, "I would like to try to do it, but I might end up crying." They have told me, "That's okay." Or I've said, "I would like to try to go, but I might not be able to stay." They have answered, "Whenever you feel you have to go, I'll take you home." During one lunch with a friend I said, "These lunches really help me, but how many lunches am I entitled to in this healing process?" To that she simply replied, "As many as it takes!" Every time I think of her comment, I have to laugh . . . out of joy. Here's to all my friends and all those lunches — "They worked their magic. *You're* the best!"

So, in every day's decision to *try* to move ahead, I have found that God also used my efforts to bless those days; bless them with many things that can only come from the vitality of the here and now. Seeing this happen again and again, makes me want to get up and try another day. Eventually, it becomes a healthy pattern of motion that allows me more and more investment in the world as a *renewed* personality; a personality prepared for the continuation of *my* life.

Did You Miss Your Son, God?

Did You miss Your Son, God,
The way I miss mine
When Yours descended
To earth?
Was there a painful void
In the heavenly fold
When You allowed for His mortal birth?
Did You long
To talk to Jesus at times,
To have Him there
By Your side?
That's how I feel,
Since my son
Came to You,
Though I gave him
With loving pride.

Kathryn Hardgrove Popio
November 8, 1988
8:10 a.m.

7
The Next To The Last Chapter

Eleanor Roosevelt not only lost a child to illness, but she had a mother-in-law who hindered her grief work by making her feel it was unhealthy to display sorrow *at all*. So, Eleanor went into the bathroom, ran water and flushed the toilet to conceal her sobbing episodes. Fortunately, she was not only a strong woman, but a wise one. She knew grief had to be dealt with. She was one of the grief-recovery success stories mainly because she reckoned with it, taking charge of its manifestation as well as its conclusion. She took responsibility for her feelings — what she needed and what she didn't need — instead of moving with opinions of others.

We have learned a great deal about the grieving process since her time, just as we have learned more about other issues of mental health. Yet, her example in grief, as in other aspects of her life, is noteworthy. We, as individual people recovering from grief, must decide (as much as we are capable) how we will think about a multitude of things in the future; even though the future doesn't seem like it will ever be worthy of our attention again. If we don't do this for ourselves, we are relinquishing the responsibility to anything or anybody else who happens to step in to do it for us.

I had to decide, for example, how much effort was possible to put into celebrating each holiday. We had supportive family and friends who invited us to be with them or offered to come and be with us. Although they offered, I still had to decide upon an attitude for each of those days. Mac's attitude had always been to enjoy every day as much as possible. I certainly would not be doing anything for his memory or for myself if I didn't at least *try* to participate.

It was not *easy* for anybody. I set the example of talking about Mac on those occasions. Some of our family couldn't, but later said it made them feel relieved that I could because he was on everybody's mind. One of the greatest gifts anyone could give to me (and many other bereaved parents have seconded this) was some mention of his life (or just the fact that he was missed).

As the bereaved mother, I had to decide on my attitude about stray comments people made to me, as well. When people said things to me like, "Of course, you'll never be the same again," it resounded like such a pronouncement of doom that it made me rebel inside. I couldn't accept that opinion. Immediately, I called upon all the Grace I have been given to hold up as proof that God does intend to heal me that I may be restored to participate in life to the fullest capacity. I learned a great deal about life, friendship and love through my children. Therefore, how could my life in the future *not* reflect that *abundant richness*?

It will be different, to be sure. *I will never stop missing my McCall in every venture undertaken*, and I joyfully anticipate that time when I will be reunited with him; for that will be the *last chapter* of my life. But, there have been new dimensions added to the reality I previously knew which have allowed me to value each person's life more keenly than ever. It also has made it possible to look with anticipation toward this "next to the last chapter" called the present.

Some time in the year or so before Mac left, I discussed with him and with Heather that we are not just a body and mind living in the universe. We are made up of a physical body and a mind, but we are also spiritual beings. We believed that prior to the accident. However, then, as the teacher of such a truth, I couldn't imagine the vastness of it. Now, I have had a gift of experiencing a tiny level more than that basic belief. Although I still cannot imagine the vastness of God's plan for that marvelous combination he created for each of us, I am more in awe than ever. I take this into account as I anticipate my "next to the last chapter."

My children have always known of God. We were all growing in our relationships with our Savior. We knew He demanded a lot, gave a lot, listened to us, forgave and loved us. But we also knew He is a powerful God whom man does not manipulate; nor does He manipulate his children as if we were nothing more than puppets. Our freedom from such manipulation is also part of His plan. He set the universe and all of creation in motion, and all of creation may move about living their lives as free entities. Therefore, sometimes we get sick, sometimes we have accidents, and we eventually come to the end of our existence and die. Hence, we may act without regard for God or anyone else. On the other hand, we also may choose to open ourselves to His guidance, inspiration and teaching; thereby, in every circumstance, we may know strength, love, forgiveness and peace that is beyond human comprehension.

Since this is what I have come to believe, I cringe when people blame God for all their misfortunes or even credit Him as a benevolent genie of sorts for what amounts to more luck-of-the-draw than anything else. I have come to feel, through all that has happened, that God feels sad about misfortunes in our lives right along with us. His perfect will would most likely be all-harmony and all-love, but then . . . that's heaven! Then there is also His permissive will that allowed His own son to be delivered up to the cross. We must remember, too, that Jesus *could have* arranged to leap off the mountain safely in a tremendous show of almighty power when the devil tempted Him to prove He was the Son of God. But, as a human being, Jesus refused to tempt the laws of the universe; which makes me realize all the more that God does not change His laws for anyone.

Through His Grace, I believe He did open an existing channel of communication that, as human beings, we are not usually capable of perceiving. That dimension is quite real, in my estimation. I am not the only one to experience God's compassion in reaching out to comfort His children. The more I have talked with others in grief situations, the more I have come to believe such benevolence is open to us all. God's act of Grace in allowing Macaulay to play a part in creating an awareness of our spiritual reality is also a part of His magnificent plan. I did nothing to *deserve* such a gift of Grace. Mac did nothing to *deserve* to be part of it either. We are believers. That is our only part. Period. There is a reason for allowing it, however, and I am thankful for it.

It is my hope in sharing these experiences that they will also help someone else work through to a better resolution of their sorrow. Since many people clip lists and put them on their refrigerators rather than sitting down and studying someone else's experiences and advice, here is my list:

Paving The Road To A Fine Healing

 1. Take time to tell *God* how you are feeling each day.
 2. Gently pace yourself.
 3. Place inspirational items around that help uplift you.
 4. Reach out to others as much as your nature allows.
 5. Approach grief peaks with caution and courage.
 6. Enter activities in small doses.
 7. Chart reasonable short-termed goals to accomplish.
 8. Provide things on your calendar to look forward to.
 9. Be understanding with the rest of the world.
10. Shut down your cares at the end of each day by decidedly placing yourself in God's healing peace.

In looking back over the past three years, I repeatedly rejoice in the heart's rest received through a combination of actively grieving and, at the same time, striving to participate in daily issues of life. Neither has been easy. But it has been my experience to discover that God cares very deeply and reaches out to help with my burdens. I have further realized that he not only comforts me for that initial moment of communion with Him, but he compliments that comfort with incentives that move me forward from where I am. I urge anyone who is hurting to take a chance on reaching out to God. It's impossible to know how much He can do unless you have the experience yourself.

There have been so many episodes of comforting assurance, of healing and incentives to move onward that I would need another book to describe them all. Heather has urged me to share something with you here, and I do so to illustrate how God desires to uplift us all, if we will let Him.

Mac's birth date falls in August, the same month as the accident; therefore, the first year after he left us, August loomed ahead like an overwhelming monster. Because of the pain associated with the accident and his never having another birthday, it seemed August could never, ever, have the nerve to appear on the calendar again. I couldn't plan on how to cope with *those* two dates, it seemed *so* impossible. I didn't even *think* about August, because any thought in that direction was too painful.

Well, my birthday falls at the end of July, and Heather took me to a movie that day. While we were sitting in the theater, I received this message in my inner heart — "I'm with you, Mom."

It was as simple as that; yet vivid enough to draw my attention from the movie. The message continued being a part of my consciousness throughout August . . .

"I'm with you, Mom."

If I needed it thirty times a day, I had it . . .

"I'm with you, Mom."

Whenever I felt weak, the message came to me and rekindled my spirit so completely that I was constantly amazed as well as uplifted. I can't explain any of these experiences, and

I don't try. In Matthew, chapter 18, Jesus promised us this: "Truly, I say to you, whatever you bind on earth shall be bound in heaven." I accept that promise as part of God's benevolent gift in tying love on earth to love in heaven, and I give thanks for each episode of His Grace and Mercy in my life.

Several of my close friends said they would come and spend Mac's birth date with me. One friend came in the morning and had lunch with me, and I invited the other friend to have a birthday supper with us. I found it to be a day I could truly rejoice about; rejoice that that was the anniversary of my son's arrival in my life! Several others called me to say they were thinking of me that day and were totally surprised by my joyful attitude. The wonderful thing about it was that it was a genuine joy; not something I was trying to effect for my friends.

Right before supper, one of Mac's buddies came by with his mother to bring a bouquet of flowers. I received him with great thanksgiving, and we used the flowers on our supper table. I was thrice thankful I could meet Mac's friend with a happy countenance rather than being slumped in a heap feeling sorry for myself.

As I have asked God for help and experienced that magnificent way He ignites my spirit through every effort I make, I have eventually realized the incentive to *step outside my grief*. For every step I have taken toward one goal after another and adjusting to the world's flow again, I have found some more beautiful and fulfilling experiences. How magnificent to know that a fulfilling life is possible for one so bereaved.

Additional Readings

1. Getting Through the Night, Finding Your Way After the Loss of a Loved One. By Eugenia Price, 1982; The Dial Press, New York 10017. (Reinforces vitality still existing between you and loved one.)

2. The Lonely House, Strength For Times of Loss. By Lowell Erdall, 1989; C.S.S. Publishing Co., Lima, OH 45804. (16 weeks of inspirational readings that address vital mourning issues.)

3. Helping Children Cope With Separation And Loss. By Claudia Jewett, 1982; Harvard Common Press, Boston, MA 02118. (Recognizing many guises of children's grief; provides steps for working through various types of losses.)

4. Recovering From the Loss of a Child. By Katherine Fair Donnelly, 1982; Macmillan Pub. Co., Inc., NY 10022. (Compilation of many parents' experiences; includes list of support groups.)

5. Cries From The Heart. By Margaret Spiess, 1991; Baker House, Grand Rapids, MI 49506. (Poems that capsulize thoughts of every parent who has lost a child.)

6. *No Time For Goodbyes, Coping With Sorrow, Anger, and Injustices After A Tragic Loss.* By Janice Harris Lord, 1987; Pathfinder Publishing, Ventura, CA 93003. (Counsels steps for active involvement in coping with justice system, seeking victim assistance, and understanding unique elements of sudden loss.)

7. *The Light Beyond.* Raymond Moody, M.D., 1988; Bantam Books, NY 10103. (Research reflecting existence of life after death.)

8. *No Pat Answers, Looking Squarely at Life's Most Difficult Questions.* By Eugenia Price, 1991; Doubleday, NY 10103. (Examines views in the light of real life experiences.)

9. *Tiger Tim.* By Don A. Fultz, 1991; Fairway Press, Lima, OH 45804. (Father relates family's unity in coping with boy's cancer and eventual death.)

10. *Praying Our Goodbyes.* By Joyce Rupp, OSM, 1988; Ave Marie Press, Notre Dame, IN 46556. (Theological and psychological reflections toward continuing life after losing someone.)

11. *Go Toward the Light.* By Chris Oyler, 1988; Harper and Row, Pub., NY. (Family helps child face departure from life with them.)

12. *The Mourning After, How to Manage Grief Wisely.* By Stanley P. Cornils, 1990; R & E Pub., Saratoga, CA 95070. (Discusses manifestions of grieving and recovering.)